BRIDGIT EMBE

MAKE HER SCREAM
EROTIC FANTASIES THAT SATISFY YOUR NEEDS!

Descrierea CIP a Bibliotecii Naţionale a României
BRIDGIT EMBERS
   Make Her Scream. Erotic Fantasies That Satisfy Your
Needs! / Bridgit Embers. – Bucureşti: Editura My Ebook, 2017
   ISBN 978-606-983-475-6

BRIDGIT EMBERS

MAKE HER SCREAM
EROTIC FANTASIES THAT
SATISFY YOUR NEEDS!

My Ebook Publishing House
Bucharest, 2017

Chapter 1

When Amelia Durnen walked into my office one Saturday morning I knew I was going to make the front page of all the tabloids. Her every move attracted the press, she'd had more coverage than the potato famine and was better know that the Taoiseach or the President of Ireland.

From the age of sixteen, when she ran away to Europe with her tutor, through her four marriages to some of the wealthiest men in the world, she'd been the darling of the press corps. Even climbing out of her Rolls in downtown Dublin would attract half a dozen photographers fighting to give their readers a faint glimpse of her panties. She was a celebrity without compare.

Obviously, someone of her breeding would find my office both tasteless and untidy and she didn't waste any time telling me that it looked like a shithole.

"I like it that way," I said, "it's got atmosphere,"

"But is there anywhere I can sit without the risk of serious contamination?" she asked with a faint sardonic smile on her face.

I quickly moved Snowy my cat off of the sofa, dusted a spot with my hand and suggested she sat down. She turned down my offer of coffee and instead pointed to my bottle of Jack Daniels and inquired if I had a clean glass.

As we sat sipping our Kentucky Bourbon, it was hard to focus on what she was telling me because my eyes were riveted to her long nylon clad legs. And when she bent over, attempting to find an empty spot on the coffee table to place her empty glass, I got a view of those magnificent mammary glands that had been fondled by some of the most influential men in the world.

The Durnen family, as would be expected, lived in one of the most beautiful castles in Ireland and until recently Amelia lived there with her extended family. However, one by one they had suffered unfortunate and fatal accidents. Or, so it seemed.

Although the press had attributed the fatalities to the curse of Dundurnen Castle, and the Gardai had found nothing suspicious about the deaths, she was not convinced.

"My grandfather tripped on the stone steps at the front of the house and died from a skull fracture," she said, "then my mother ran into one of the stone gateposts with her car and a few weeks later my father drove his Land Rover into a lake on the estate. The Gardai had the effrontery to suggest that he was so distraught over my mother and his father, he committed suicide."

Tears were beginning to run down her cheeks as she said that apart from the twelve servants she was now all alone at Dundurnen. I offered her my handkerchief but she politely refused it and rummaged through her purse for a tissue.

"Mr. Killeen," she said, after taking a deep breath, "I'd like you to come and stay at the castle and investigate these deaths, I refuse to believe they were all accidental."

Before I agreed to take on the case I asked if there had been any attempts on her life. She shook her head. Then I asked who'd benefit if she died. She shuddered at the thought but then said it would go to her brother who was somewhere in South America helping the poor.

"Didn't he inherit under your father's will?"

"Well, father didn't really have any money I've subsidized the estate for years, thanks to my four ex-husbands."

"But didn't he get a share of the estate itself?"

"No, father left that all to me, he knew Crispin would want to sell it and put the money in the charitable trust that he runs. Father didn't have anything against the poor but the castle has been in the family for hundreds of years. He wanted to keep it that way."

She went on to explain that she hadn't seen her brother for several years and had little contact until she hired an old friend of his as a gardener.

"What do you know about this gardener?"

"Oh Tatham's OK, he does a good job and is always respectful."

"Did he have a letter of introduction from your brother?"

"Better than that he had a couple of photographs of him and Crispin together, they lived in some remote village high in the Peruvian rain forest, teaching the Indians improved methods of cultivation."

"So your brother's an expert in agriculture?"

"Oh yes, he studied at in England and America before he took off."

"And who finances him?"

"Well he had some money of his own but Tatham did say he was running a bit low and so I sent some funds to an address he gave me.

"Did you receive a reply?"

"Yes – he went to the nearest town and emailed me. But what has this got to do with the deaths at Dundurnen?"

"I just like to get as much background material as possible before I take a job on."

"So you'll come out to the castle and stay for a few days?"

"I'll be there this evening," I said.

She arose from the chair, shook my hand in the most ladylike way and left the room like a graceful Gazelle. I poured myself another drink and I sat thinking about those long legs and what it would feel like to have them wrapped around my back. Eventually, I had to return to earth, where I flung a few things into a travel bag and drove the 50 K or so to Dundurnen.

I was ushered into the impressive edifice by Yeats the butler and on to the west terrace where cucumber sandwiches and Oolong Tea were awaiting my pleasure. Amelia, wearing a long flowing gown invited me to sit down. Just for the fun of it, I did examine the cups for cleanliness before she played mother. My sense of humor was not wasted on her and she gave a little smile.

"You seemed very interested in my brother Mr. Killeen and so I've pulled out the two photos for you to look at."

I scrutinized them carefully. Crispin, a good looking young man with a strained smile on his face was flanked by Phillip Tatham on one side and a man she identified as Joe Mulligan on the other.

"He's another friend of my brother," she said, "they're all involved with the same project."

I took out my trusty magnifying glass for a closer look and I got one of my pings, the little noise that goes off in my head when I think I've made a significant discovery. In this case, studying the background in the photographs it looked a bit like our three young NGO workers were in some sort of prison. Not the modern barred structure that we're used to seeing but possible a local rural lock-up.

After we'd polished off those delicately prepared sandwiches Amelia took me out to see the scene of each accident. I took a few measurements and some photos and then we returned to the house for dinner. I told her that I didn't have anything particularly dressy and she said that a T-shirt and blazer looked good on me and not to worry.

"That's your style," she said, "don't change it on my account."

I washed up in the beautifully appointed room I'd been assigned and when the gong sounded and I emerged onto the landing I discovered that my equally beautiful host was my next door neighbor. And I also discovered that she had a sense of humor, as she was wearing a very short mini-skirt and high heels topped off with a T-shirt and blazer.

"How do I look," she asked twirling around.

"Like every woman in the world should look I smiled," as she took me by the arm and escorted me down the marble staircase to the dining room.

To say the table looked elegant, or even opulent would have been an understatement. The china, the glassware and the monogrammed cutlery could have graced the tables of the crown heads of Europe without embarrassment.

The two of us were seated close together and not at opposing ends like one often sees in cartoons. And during dinner, which was accompanied with an excellent bottle of 1990 Domaine de la Romanee-Conti, we shot the shit and laughed a good deal.

Retiring to the drawing room for coffee and liqueur, she sat next to me on the overstuffed sofa and suddenly became quite serious.

"Do you think my family members were murdered?" she asked.

"I think it's a distinct possibility."

"Do you think I could be next on the list?"

I said that was also a possibility and she went strangely quiet.

"Who would benefit from your death apart from your brother?" I inquired, trying to attract her attention, as her mind seemed to have wandered off somewhere.

"Nobody," she mumbled, and then realizing the implications she looked me straight in the eye and yelled, "you're not suggesting Crispin would kill off all the people he loves to gain the estate are you?"

I explained that I always started my inquiries by including every eventuality no matter how remote, gradually eliminating one possibility at a time. She calmed down and changed the subject as though she couldn't cope with any more unpleasant suggestions.

"The woman who gave me your name described you as a great detective and an extraordinary lover, she smiled, "do you make it a practice to seduce all of your clients?"

"Only the females," I replied, flippantly.

"So you admit having an eye for the ladies."

"I admire beauty."

"And how did I score when I walked into your office."

"Eleven out of ten."

"I should be flattered."

"No – I should be flattered that you chose me to help you with your problem."

"Do you know what my problem is right now?" she asked, moving her face so close to mine I could feel her hot breath on my cheek, " I'm feeling awfully horny."

With that, she gently touched my lips with hers and then withdrew, as if to say, "Your move."

Although I had a hard on that had driven my foreskin all the way back to my balls I decided to savor every moment of this encounter. Rushing things would have been like serving a vintage wine in a shot glass. I wanted to take my time and so I placed my hand on her leg and moved the hem of her skirt back to expose her lacy panties that barely covered her crack.

Her body went stiff for a moment. With my left hand still on her thigh, I used my right to slip up her Tshirt where I made contact with her soft warm tits. I rubbed my palm over her nipples and then pressed my lips against hers.

As the lady said, I'm not inexperienced in these matters but there was something about her that was very, very special. My whole body was beginning to tingle as if all my nerve endings were short circuiting. However, I didn't give in to the urge where I would have crushed my lips against hers and groped her all over.

In the end, it was Amelia that let loose and as her tongue plunged into my mouth her hand reached down and grabbed onto my cock. After that, it was a matter of tearing each other's clothes off and we ended up lying on a Bear Skin Rug rolling around naked like two sex starved teenagers. Then she suddenly broke loose and began to run around on all fours like a dog, with her tits swaying from side to side and her ass in the air just inviting penetration.

It seemed a little crazy but a piece of tail is a piece of tail and so I bounded after her like an overgrown Wolf Hound and grabbed onto her hips, dragged her back so she was in line with my dick and drove it into her. She gasped as I gave a quick thrust or two and put my arms around her holding onto her pendulous breasts. I only managed to thrust it in and out a few times when the crazy bitch broke loose and hopped onto the sofa as if she was a real dog. I just stood up and looked down at her for a few seconds, I was a little confused as to what she wanted it was then that she lunged at me and took my cock into her mouth and began to suck hard. For support, I fell forward and hung onto the back of the sofa.

I was beginning to sweat as she kneaded my balls with both hands and took my dick so far into her mouth when I shot my load it must have coated her tonsils. There was no way I was going to admit it at the time but she completely shagged me out and when she stuck her ass up in the air again I had a job to get it hard enough to penetrate. However, when her warm, well-lubricated cunt wrapped around it I was ready to pound her pussy with a vengeance but that's when the butler came into the room.

"Can I get you anything before I retire madam?" he asked, appearing to be oblivious to the fact that I had my dick stuck up her.

"No I think that will be all – thank you Yeats. "

As he left the room, she suddenly yelled: "Fuck me Paddy and fill me up with cum."

I was a bit hesitant as I thought the gardener might suddenly appear asking if he should prune the roses in the morning. As we did seem to be alone at last, and by now I was a little frustrated I grabbed onto her tits really hard and I pounded her cunt as if I was cleaning a rat's nest out of a pipe. She loved it and two hours later I was allowed to retire with my cock feeling as though it had been in a meat grinder.

The next morning during breakfast I asked her at what time of the day the dubious accidents occurred, she told me they all happened after dark. Suddenly I got another one of my pings and I hurriedly finished my coffee and made for the building where all the garden tools and supplies were kept. I searched it thoroughly and high on a shelf I found what I was looking for, it was a laser gun. I had a feeling that our man Tatham had hidden and laid in wait for the so called accident victims and blinded them with the laser as they drove on the estate. In the case of the grandfather, he had concealed himself in the nearby bashes and then flashed the light in his eyes as he was about to descend the steps.

My next job was to examine those photographs where I thought her brother looked under duress; I then phoned Wanda, my landlady, whose past experience serving with an Italian Intelligence Agency came in useful from time to time. I asked her to do some checking with the Peruvian authorities. and spent the rest of the morning checking the accident locations again and then it was time for an elegant lunch with Amelia.

She asked me if I was making any progress and I told her I was.

"So you don't think they were accidents?" she cried, excitedly.

"No, I don't," I replied, "and I don't want you to drive in the dark until this case is solved."

She looked absolutely terrified but then asked me once again if I was suggesting her brother was involved. When I said I wasn't sure she got quite angry and told me that the whole idea of him wanting to kill off the family members one by one was preposterous.

"He's not even in the country," she said, "how could he be responsible?"

"I don't think we can prove where he is at the moment but we do know he has a friend here."

"You mean Tatham?" she gasped, "Mr. Killeen I think you are letting your imagination run wild."

"I didn't tell her about the laser gun I'd found because I couldn't prove it was Tatham's. The tool shed had no lock on it, consequently, anyone could have concealed it there, although he was my prime suspect.

My accusations seemed to send her into a moody silence and that was good because I really needed to concentrate on the job at hand. We had a quiet supper together and then slipped back into Dun Laoghaire to consult with Wanda, who told me she'd uncovered some important information.

She was still in my office where she'd been using my computer and phone. When I got there she reported that she'd managed to trace him through his charity website, which included a phone number. Amelia had never mentioned having seen a website, I guess she'd never had time between marriages and lovers to look it up.

Wanda got her husband to speak to him in Irish, "He didn't even recognize the language," she said. Of course lots of Irish people don't speak the language fluently but they usually have a smattering, apparently, he didn't have one word. She had concluded that she was speaking to someone pretending to be Crispin. Probably the recipient of the money Amelia sent. She handed me a file she put together and I headed back to the castle.

I didn't want to jump to any conclusions until I'd asked my client about her brother's language skills. However, when I got back she wasn't there. Yeats told me that she'd received a call from her brother who had arrived at Dublin Airport from South America. I didn't have her cell number to call her but I thought I could prevent yet another accident by taking possession of the laser. Unfortunately, it was gone. It looked like Tatham had gotten there first.

I had intended to talk to my suspect and other members of the staff the following day so I'd not actually seen him apart from the photo that Amelia had. Now he was out there presumably waiting for her to come home when she realized her brother wasn't there. That could have taken hours.

I figured he wouldn't want to commit another killing on the property and I racked my brain for a location between the estate and Dublin that would be ideal for another accident. There was a very dangerous bend in the road about 5 kilometers away and I decided to take a look at that. When I asked Yeats what kind of car Tatham drove he said he didn't have a car, he rode a motorcycle.

Heading out towards the location I slowly scoured the bend and sure enough, there was a bike tucked in beside some trees and in the shadows, I saw a man I presumed to be Tatham. When I stopped the car he looked in a bit of a panic and quickly climbed on his bike but I managed to run alongside him as he pulled out onto the road and I punched him in the side of the head as hard as I could. He and his fancy dancy machine skidded across the road and almost got hit by an oncoming vehicle.

Tatham would have got up but he couldn't, I had to drag him to my car, where I bundled him into the back seat and put the cuffs on him. Back at the castle, I gagged my prisoner to stop him calling out and then I dumped him in the tool shed and waited for Amelia to return.

I really didn't have anything on the accused that would stand up in court until I searched his room and found three false passports, a gun and a quantity of drugs. I presented these to the Gardai, along with the laser gun and hoped that they would be able to make a case stick against him. Presuming her brother was dead and Tatham's colleague had assumed his identity, hoping to inherit the family fortune, my client wanted me to go to Peru with her but I had other commitments. In the end, I persuaded her to take my friend Michael Noiseaux along, he spoke Spanish and French and had a martial arts background. He was the perfect international traveling companion.

Three weeks later, after working things out with the Peruvian authorities, Michael returned. He was pale and worn from his ordeal, as he had shared a room with Amelia for the whole time he was away. The other two Michaels and myself, wanting to listen to his sexual exploits, and perhaps restore the color to his cheeks, plied him with enough Guinness to float a battleship. He does claim that she offered him a permanent job as her personal assistant but he didn't think running around naked on all fours was quite the position he was looking for.

Chapter 2

Gill Wingham preyed on vulnerable women. He was mostly unemployed and didn't have a pot to piss in and yet he spent a good part of each year in some tropical paradise.

His methodology was simple, he went all out to find some lonely plain Jane who looked as if she might have a few bucks and from there on it was easy. On their first dates, he would apologize for being strapped for funds but he would struggle to pay his share. After two or three dates he'd use his highly successful stock phrase, "If I had the money I'd take you to some tropical get-a-way and make love to you every day to the sound of the surf."

In 75% of cases, the woman would suggest that she could pay for such a holiday and off they'd go to Aruba, Cancun or Rio and fuck the days away. This enabled Gill to eat well, drink all the booze he could handle and lounge around in the sun flirting with some of the other girls. Some years he managed to squeeze in up to four such vacations. Of course, when they returned home he would simply explain to his weeping victim that they were simply incompatible.

Living in a small city it was inevitable that word would get around but Gill was simply too stupid to think about that. The hairdresser for two of his "Sugar-Dollies" was intrigued that their stories were so similar and when she told them her suspicions it started the ball rolling for some sweet revenge.

After making some inquiries they found three more plain Janes who'd been duped and dumped by the lascivious lounge lizard. Put five very bitter young women together and you've got trouble. Morag, a woman who had spent three Martinique weeks with his cock in her mouth, was particularly vengeful.

"We should really nail this bastard," she said, "He needs to be taught a lesson."

Although it sounded like an appropriate punishment, after due consideration, "cutting off his balls," was rejected as being a little extreme. However, Sabena came up with another method of emasculating him that sounded like fun.

"I have a friend who's a professional dominatrix, why don't we chip in some cash and set them up for a vacation together. I think she could make it hell for him."

The idea was met with a round of applause and it was arranged for Helga, the woman in question, to call on his apartment to do a survey for her Daddy's business and bait the trap. Sure enough, Gill fell for it hook, line and sinker. And after just one date Helga suggested taking off for some exclusive resort for a two-week live-in and he nodded his head so enthusiastically it nearly fell off.

Once on the isolated island of Yarabuko Helga began to show her true colors. As soon as they got into their room, ironically numbered 69, she slipped off her clothes revealing her black leather panties and bra. He was, to say the least, a little surprised by her choice of underwear. Then came the whip – she produced it from her luggage and smashed it a couple of times on the dressing table.

"What's that for," he stammered nervously, "Are you thinking of going riding or something?"

"I'm going to ride you, you horrible little turd because you are now my love-slave for a whole two weeks."

Gill swallowed hard and even managed to force a smile, "Is this some kind of a joke."

"Do you see me laughing?" she retorted, giving his buttocks a clip with the end of her whip, "Now strip off and get on all fours."

It was only natural for him to be a little hesitant but he soon started to peel off his gear in response to another stinging clip from her crop.

Once naked and on all fours, she climbed on his back and rode him around the room. His knees were sore and he was exhausted by the time she'd finished her little canter. When she dismounted she didn't let him get up but stood before him and stripped off her panties to reveal a substantial bush.

"Now lick it until I cum," she yelled.

"Shouldn't we shower first," he asked cringing in case she delivered another blow.

"Take it as it is – or ain't you man enough?"

Even a sniveling, cowardly gigolo like Gill doesn't like to have his masculinity challenged and so he moved up to her crotch, opened up her lips with his trembling fingers and inserted his tongue.

"Now lick it and lick it good," she cried.

Being a dominatrix doesn't mean you're immune to a little sexual pleasure and putting aside his contemptible personality, her licker was a pretty good looking dude. As his tongue glided up and down her wet crack she began to tingle all over and tugged on his hair as she could feel her quim going into seismic overload.

As her orgasm lasted for some two and a half minutes, her long-tongued love slave found his face being smashed repeated into her oozing grove and he was finding it increasingly difficult to breathe. When she let his hair go he collapsed onto the carpet completely fucked.

For Gill, every day proved to be more hellish than the next. As it was her plastic that was paying for everything he was not allowed to drink alcohol and while she dined on 12-ounce steaks and lobster thermidor he was restricted to egg salads and the occasional Spanish omelet.

Back in the bedroom, the torment continued. She would wake him at three o'clock in the morning and force him to jerk himself off over her tits. Most nights he slept sardine style with his ankles manacled to the bed head and his face in her muff.

After the first week, Gill was beginning to show signs of cracking. He even considered trying to swim the hundred mile shark infested stretch of sea to the mainland. When that seemed a little impractical he turned his attention to the fattest, ugliest girl at that resort hoping he could con her into flying them both out of there – but she turned out to be a Lesbian. Eventually, he broke down and cried and Helga began to feel sorry for him.

After phoning the girls it was decided that the punishment had gone on long enough and to let him spend the last few days in relative normality. That night in the restaurant, with one eye twitching nervously, he waited for his egg salad to be served. However, he perked up considerably when she ordered steaks for two and a bottle of very good wine. As he dug ravenously into the juicy Porterhouse and sipped on his 2009 Bordeaux, he couldn't help but think this could be his "last meal."

Perhaps she was planning to kill him by sexual over-stimulation; after all, there was no law that said you couldn't fuck a man to death. "But why was she doing this?" that was the question he kept asking himself. In the end, he thought that perhaps she been let down by some scurrilous cad and she was now taking out revenge on all men.

He became even more confused when that night she put on some slinky lingerie, a few dabs of perfume and proceeded to kiss him passionately. It was difficult for him to respond because at any moment he expected her to pull a whip out of her cunt and begin to beat on his balls with it, or something equally insidious. However, instead of being confronted with "Helga the Terrible," she became loving and sensitive and went down on him.

He'd had his cock sucked many times before but not the way she did it. She slid it between her full lips deep into her throat and twirled her tongue around it at the same time. When his cum started to move up his pipe he yelled out because he feared more punishment if he came in her mouth, but she sucked every drop out of him and swallowed it.

For the next few days he licked her body from head to toe, pounded her pussy and fucked her face, and it was heavenly. In spite of the great sex, when it was time to check out he wasn't really sorry to say goodbye to room 69, but then he was not aware what awaited him back home.

Helga went with him to the apartment and when they opened the door there was a big surprise, the five relatively unattractive girls all sat there waiting for him. Forcing him down into a chair, his former victims offered him a deal. They would pay his rent, buy his food and a reasonable amount of liquor in exchange for him satisfying their sexual needs according to a schedule they'd drawn up.

"You'll have to do whatever we say," said, one.

"No matter how bizarre," stipulated another.

Gill protested, saying that such a deal was beneath his dignity but when Helga produced her whip and started to lick the end of it, he decided that it might be a reasonable arrangement. His only stipulation was that he was allowed to have a few days rest to recoup from his holiday with Helga.

Chapter 3

The moment the Rev Michael Fitzgerald graduated from theological college he was gung-ho to take on the sinners of the world. However, he was a little disappointed that instead of being getting this own church right away he was given the assignment to assist another minister over the Christmas period.

"It's a very busy time and Rev. Barnes has been having some health problems," said the Bishop, I'm sure your help will be invaluable."

When he arrived at St. Emery's he was astounded to find that the minister he was to help out was a woman he'd been at school with. Although she was two years ahead of him her escapades were legendary. Nancy Barnes had been involved in everything from making home brew to letting the boys feel her tits for a dollar a head.

Her sexual expressions were described by the health teacher as "frightening," and her short skirts and plunging necklines had solicited similar comments. There was a sigh of relief when she eventually graduated and Michael was quite certain that no one would ever have suspected her of being religious.

As one of the boys who'd paid to feel her tits she recognized him right away.

"Oh my god if it isn't little Michael Fitzgerald – if you've come for another feel I have to warn you the price has gone up."

Embarrassed he tried to laugh off the comment but over the next few hours while she was giving him the grand tour and filling him on what she had planned for the festive season she brought it up several times.

It appeared that she didn't have any physical health problems she had just gone through a period of depression.

"I basically need somebody to talk to," she said, "It's so fucking boring here. There's nobody who can hold a conversation for more than five minutes without referring to the weather or the crops. I got so down in the dumps I even thought of preaching from the pulpit naked as I thought it would at least get the locals talking about something different. The Bishop, of course, was dead against it and he's sent you here to keep me company – well sort of."

"Sort of?"

"Well I suspect as soon as I've filled you in on things they'll hand over the church to you and I'll be sent as a missionary to Papua or somewhere nakedness is more readily acceptable."

"They certainly didn't say anything about taking over the church to me they just said you needed help over Christmas."

"Of course they wouldn't come straight out with it – they were probably shit scared you might turn the job down."

"Surely it can't be that bad."

"It's fucking horrible – on the days I'm not listening to their tales of incest and debauchery I just sit and drink myself into unconsciousness. Speaking of which I have a nice bottle of home brew awaiting your approval in the vestry."

"I'm not sure if that's a good idea," he said, shaking his head disapprovingly.

"Oh come on – just join me for one small drink and I might let you feel my tits for free," she laughed.

Sipping on what tasted like a mixture of benzene and turpentine he asked her what ever made her decided to take holy orders.

"My Dad's a vicar you know and he was quite sick at the time so I basically did it to please him. I would rather have been a prostitute, there's real money in that and you meet a lot of nice people but here I am and here I'll stay – at least while my Dad's still alive."

With this, she topped up Michaels glass and started to discuss the carols the choir intended to perform at the Christmas Eve service.

"They're just a bunch of old folk," she said, "kids don't want to be in choirs anymore they're too busy with their technical devices. I don't suppose I could even get them interested even if I let them feel my tits," she giggled.

Michael realizing that she'd drank far too much try to persuade her to go back to the parish house. "You probably think because we're going to be in the house together you're going to fuck me," she said, her speech getting a little slurred, "Well you might at that," and with this, she started to laugh hysterically.

Nancy took his arm and almost dragged him out of the Church, across the graveyard and into the house that was close by. The moment she got through the front door she stripped off her clothes and started to dance around.

"Take yours off too," she cried, "Let's be like Adam and Eve – they weren't ashamed of their bodies."

Out of her cassock, she certainly didn't have anything to be ashamed of either – she had a great figure, lovely firm tits, long shapely legs and a neatly trimmed pussy. In spite of trying to resist temptation, he was developing a hard-on and decided that he'd better find his room and unpack while he still had some self-control left.

It was a narrow winding staircase and she led the way with her lovely bare ass moving in the most provocative way. When they arrived at the top of the stairs he realized too late that she had strategically placed a bunch of mistletoe over the bedroom door. Soon her full lips were clamped to his and her tongue was half way down his throat.

Having a suitcase in either hand he couldn't do much about it. When he did drop them and let them go crashing down the stairs it didn't help matters. Before you could say cock sucking mother fucker she dropped to her knees, unzipped his flies and had slipped his dick in her mouth. He wanted to protest but it was too late – he was enjoying it.

Nancy really knew how to work her mouth around it, she didn't just go up and down she used her lips and tongue creatively until he felt his cum rushing up his pipe.

"Oh god – I'm cumming," he cried out.

She gave a few more sucks taking it right up to the last minute and then moved back and worked it with her hand as it shot out all over her face. With his cum dripping from the end of her nose she told him he owed her a turn, with this, she rushed into his room, threw herself on the bed and opened up her legs. Michael knew he was breaking every rule in the book but it didn't seem right to leave a lady twitching with expectation on the bed and just turn your back on her.

Kneeling at the foot of the bed he pulled her legs forward until his mouth was tight against her wet crack.

"Holy shit," she yelled as his tongue began to probe inside her pussy lips, "Holy shit."

Michael loved the taste of it and he kept licking and licking and until she screamed and jerked her ass up and down on the bed as if she was going into a convulsion. He was dying to suck those tits he'd felt when he was a young man and he straddled her body and bent down to take her hardened nipples into his mouth. Nancy was in ecstasy moaning and groaning and throwing her arms around in complete abandonment.

She became even louder when he moved up and rubbed his dick all over her perky tits. It was now hard enough to shove into her love tunnel and so he moved her into position so that he could kneel between her legs and then he rammed it in – a hole in one.

Nancy gasped and threw her arms back as he withdrew it and with the same precision rammed it back in again. Soon he was driving it in fast and furious with his balls banging together like Christmas bells – only silent. The sight of her voluptuous tits bouncing around just seemed to inspire him to go faster and faster until he gave a primeval yell and shot his load deep inside of her.

To cut a long Christmas story short they fucked each other right through to the New Year until they were caught doing it in the vestry by an influential churchwarden. Once their behavior was reported to the Bishop, they were equipped with mosquito nets and sun tan lotion and put on a plane to Papua. The little mission they run is up in the jungle-covered mountains and the only thing either of them ever wears is a dog collar and the locals love them and they love each other. Almost every night!

Chapter 4

Ray Mallender had a couple months break from university and he wanted to do something exciting for at least part of it. Serving fast food was out of the question and so was construction, he'd been there and done that and he didn't want to do it again. He searched several papers in Wales where he lived but there was nothing that took his fancy. However one day on the train from Cardiff to Aberystwyth he picked up a newspaper that someone had left behind and there was an advert for an assistant to help with a research project at a bird sanctuary off the coast of Scotland.

After a rather in-depth, and somewhat personal interview on Skype with Professor Marian McLeod, who had posted the ad, he secured the job and arrived at Portree on the Isle of Skye for their first actual meeting. She turned out to be a very good looking lady, probably in her mid-thirties, with a great set tits tucked under a heavy sweater and wearing a kilt and knee socks. Her hair was taken back like a librarian and her thick horn-rimmed glasses kind of added to that persona.

After exchanging greetings he carried his back pack and sleeping bag on board a creaky old fishing boat while the captain and his mate loaded a number of boxes and barrels of fuel.

"We've got to carry lots of supplies," she said, "We might get cut off for an extra couple of weeks, the weather is very unpredictable where we're going."

He was already getting quite nervous about spending three weeks with Marian but the idea of that being extended was really scary. She seemed a dull, serious kind of woman who was probably not going to play Frisbee with him and would more than likely work late into the night. In a bizarre sort of way, he was very close to the truth.

When they arrived on the island, that looked awfully small and virtually covered with seabirds, he caught sight of their accommodation as they came into the shelter of a rocky cove. It was an abandoned lighthouse.

Hauling the provisions and fuel up the cliffs with a hand operated wooden crane was heavy going, then they had to be loaded on a trolley and pushed up a steep incline to a storage shed. He was completed bushed by the time they got into the living quarters that didn't look that bad at first glance.

Marian, obviously seeing that he looked tired, told him to sit down while she made some tea and sandwiches. She whipped off her heavy sweater and let her unrestricted tits sway from side to side as she moved around the kitchen area.

When she laid the table she stuck a bottle of Scotch in the middle telling him they could have a wee dram in their tea. It turned out that she had a wee dram of tea in her whiskey and after a few of these she loosened up quite a bit.

There was only one bedroom and only one bed.

"They're used to be three in here when the lighthouse was operating," she said, "But they moved out a lot of the stuff when it closed, much of what you see here now is mine. I come out a couple of times a year to do my research and to write and so I do need a few creature comforts."

As she started to make up the bed she turned to him as he stood by the door, "You can put your sleeping bag over there on the sheepskin rug, or you can sleep in the bed with me if you're not too shy."

Ray didn't know what to say and just ended up gibbering like an idiot. She certainly didn't look his type until she returned from the bathroom just wearing a baggy T-shirt and with her hair flowing down on her shoulders.

"Have you made up your mind about the sleeping arrangements," she asked climbing into bed showing him right up her long shapely sock free legs as she did so.

"Well – I'd prefer to sleep in the bed of course but I'm afraid I couldn't control myself."

"Neither could I," she said, "So if that's your only problem – jump in."

He took off his pants carefully and was going to leave his shirt and underwear on but Marian stopped him in his tracks.

"If you're planning to fuck me, young man, I suggest you take off all of your clothes and with this, she sat up and peeled off her baggy t-shirt exposing what he thought were the most beautiful tits he'd ever seen.

When he did strip off she raised her eyebrows when she saw his dick. He wasn't sure whether she thought it to be satisfactory or not, so he was still a bit self-conscious as he climbed in beside her. Once he was under the covers she just turned her back on him and shoved her bum into his groin area. It looked as if she thought he should make the first moves.

Ray put his arm over her and cupped one of her tits in his hand, she wiggled her ass a bit as if it was a seal of approval. He rubbed the nipple and saw that it was erect and had the urge to take it into his mouth. However when he tried to turn her over she resisted a bit so it became a sort of wrestling match with him eventually straddling her body so that he could suck those delicious looking fun bags.

She let him nibble on them for a while and arched her back as though she was thoroughly enjoying it and then without warning, she shoved him off of her. Ray was a bit confused but he was not put off, his dick was as hard and as straight as a flagpole and he was dying to cum so as she'd turned her back on him once more he tried to slip it in her bum. She wriggled a bit as if she might be facilitating his move but then resumed her former position almost fracturing his treasured possession.

Ray didn't know what to make of her behavior, he was getting frustrated and so he threw all of the covers off of the bed jumped off himself. Kneeling down on the floor he grabbed her ankles and drew her down towards him so that he could bury his face in her hairy pussy. Even though she was groaning as he proceeded to eat her out she still struggled, making it difficult for him to move his tongue around her pink petals as he wanted to.

The next surprise came when she turned over and stuck her ass in the air. He had to reposition himself by leaning backward with his head between her legs. Then he had to struggle to get his arms free so that he could reach up to play with her dangling tits at the same time. Now she remained still and began to breathe heavy, this was followed by "OMG, Oh Fuck" and a number of other swear words and blasphemies.

When she came, she yelled out loud and she crushed her cunt hard against his face until she almost suffocated him. He was having some difficulty in breathing but kept on licking and sucking anyway. When it became too much for her to take she flopped forward onto the bed, with his tongue following her hairy muff until it was out of reach.

"You fucking bastard," she said, when she managed to raise herself up, "I'll get you for that," and she literally hauled him up on the bed by his shoulders and positioned him so that she could take his dick into her mouth. She was so carried away he was afraid she might bite it off, but she was actually gentle, sucking it as if it was a ripe banana, and tantalizing his balls with her fingers.

When Ray felt his scrotum on the boil and knew he was about to cum he warned her but she kept it in her mouth but instead of speeding it up she made it tortuously slow and it was as frustrating as hell. He was so desperate he tried to thrust it in and out of her mouth himself but then she moved back as if she might stop if he didn't behave.

When he came in her mouth it was like his whole body was going into shock. He was shaking like someone in a fit as it oozed out of his dick in short spurts. She looked up at him with her big brown eyes as she continued to drain every drop out of his balls.

Even though his dick had lost a bit of its stiffness Marian needed it now and she wanted it doggie style. She was well lubricated and so it there was no difficulty in slipping it in but then it was her that did all the movements. She wanted him to stand still while she drove her ass backward and forwards. It felt great but he had anxious to take over, what he considered to be the man's role. Alas, it seemed as if Marian had other ideas and she was not shy about enforcing them.

Before he shot his load into her love tunnel he did manage to take control and started ramming it in and out at a furious pace, holding on to her swinging tits from behind as he did so. Marian loved it and she was screaming as his balls kept colliding with her ass and he made those final rapid thrusts.

They were both exhausted at the end and just lay there naked holding hands. The next day he was expecting to go out chasing viscous seabirds but Marian said that she had a wee confession to make.

"I'm not an ornithologist," she said, "I actually write books on human sexual behavior – if you're upset because I've deceived you – feel free to leave by the next boat."

"When does that leave," he grinned wryly.

"In three weeks – possibly four."

"That sounds reasonable," he smiled, sneaking up behind her and groping her tits, "In fact, I'm hoping the weather takes a turn for the worst."

Chapter 5

When 18-year-old Damon Yates applied for a Saturday job at a fashionable women's store he didn't quite know what he was in for. Annette DuBois, the owner, born in Chicago but who had a distinct French accent, would have preferred a girl for the job but Damon's father was her therapist and so she felt kind of obligated.

"This job is for a gopher." Annette explained, "Saturday is always our Fashion Show Day and my models work very hard, so when they need anything – you go-for-it – whether it's coffee, hairspray or they need help with getting a dress on. Do you understand?"

Damon nodded, "Yes – I understand perfectly."

The models were not particularly impressed with Damon on that first day, he was skinny, wore thick glasses and his hair looked like as though he'd insulted his barber. However, he turned out to be very efficient and so towards the end of the day they warmed towards him.

It was not an easy job, every time he walked into the dressing room there would be at least one of the models with her breasts showing or walking around in a thong. He developed such a boner at one point he was having difficulty walking.

At the end of the long day, the six models sat around in various stages of nakedness and drank coffee. It was then when a girl called Jani noticed the enormous bulge in his pants.

"Look at Damon," she cried, "We've given him a boner."

The girls all laughed and then, a particularly beautiful tall, long legged model called Mahala said someone should help him with that.

"Go on – you help him Mahala," the rest of them chorused.

"Go on help him with it." laughed Jani.

Damon, who was leaning on one of the dressing tables drinking his coffee, turned beet red as Mahala advanced on him walking in the most sensuous manner. She was wearing absolutely nothing and soon Damon was confronted with a pair of perky breasts and a shaved flower rubbing up the front of his pants.

She put her hand down and gently rubbed his boner. "Would you like some help with that Damon."

He just swallowed and nodded his head as the girls in the background laughed and came up with crude remarks. Mahala began to undo his shirt with her long slender fingers and when it was off it revealed a thin bony chest that impressed absolutely no one.

When she began to unfasten his belt he became extremely nervous and started to breathe rather heavily. The girls all cheered when the buckle was undone and their colleague, with a little drama, added, unzipped his flies.

The moment his pants fell to the ground there was a gasp from all the onlookers and "Holy Shit," from Mahala.

"Look at the size of that dick," said Yvonne.

"He's got a bigger dick than my boyfriend," cried Sandy, "And he's six foot four."

They all moved in for a closer look as Mahala gently took it in her right hand while cupping his balls in the left.

"Watch out," joked Yvonne, "That thing might poke you in the eye."

"Ashley, who was normally one of the quiet ones suggested that if she got down on her knees it probably would. Mahala didn't need any more prompting. She lowered herself very slowly as Damon closed his eyes and tensed up the few muscles he had.

The girls all stood around waiting in anticipation for the moment when Mahala's ruby red lips would make contact with Damon's huge red tube. She just touched it gently with her tongue at first and his body jerked like as if he'd been shot, knocking some of the paraphernalia off of the dressing table.

"Do you want me to take the whole thing in my mouth Damon," she teased in a low sensuous voice.

He couldn't reply because his throat had gone completely dry, he just nodded, his eyes still closed and his face contorted as though he was in agony. Mahala slipped it into her mouth a little at a time. She couldn't get it all in it was just too big but she did her best.

Getting a little excited herself she dug her long fingernails into his bum as her generous lips began moving up and down his dick. He started to moan and so did she, and the girls had now stopped laughing. Yvonne began to finger herself as the action got more and more intense and Sandy and Jani fingered each other.

When Damon started to gasp that he was cumming Mahala took it out of her mouth and began to run his dick around her erect nipples. As his throbbing cock felt the softness of her tits he got tenser and tenser and then, much to the delight of the little audience, he began to yell as his cum spurted out all over her soft white skin.

She wiped some of it off with her fingers and tasted it and then the others lined up to do the same.

"That's yummy," said Yvonne, "Have you got any left.?"

Damon just sunk down to the floor having had the greatest experience of his life and felt too exhausted to say anything. Yvonne, however, who had already given herself an orgasm, was desperate to have his big dick up inside of her.

Sandy didn't think poor Damon was up for it but when Yvonne offered him her hand and pulled him to his feet they could see that his boner had returned to full strength. She took him over to a chez lounge at the side of the dressing room and asked him to lie down. His former look of apprehension had gone and he now had a faint smile on his face.

Once he was on his back with his flagpole pointing towards the ceiling she straddled his thin body and lowered herself on to him. She gasped as it went further in than she anticipated. With calls of "Ride him Cowboy," echoing in her ears the incredibly gorgeous model began to gyrate her beautiful round ass to the point where Damon's eyes looked as though they would pop out of his head.

Yvonne had to coach him a little on the way and took his hands and placed them on her tits. He was so excited he squeezed them a little too hard.

"Take it easy," she cried as she jumped up and down on his enormous stiff dick to the chant of "Fuck, fuck, fuck, fuck, fuck from the rest of them. The next thing she knew he was pushing hard on her chest as he could feel his cum forcing its way upward. His moans and the heat being created by the rapid action on her cunt sent her screaming into orgasm. The other girls cheered as Damon shot his load and took one enormous deep breath.

Yvonne was so overcome she had to be helped off of his dick. She then sat on a chair and started to laugh – "My God," that was amazing – absolutely amazing."

Damon got off the sofa and quietly put on his clothes. Sandy went over to him and put her arms around his neck and kissed him. "My turn first next week OK?"

He nodded, waved goodbye to the girls who were still crowding around Yvonne and he left, thinking that being a gopher was a pretty cool job.

CPSIA information can be obtained
at www.ICGtesting.com
Printed in the USA
BVHW041627300520
580482BV00011B/504